INCREASE
RABBIT

By T. L. McCready, Jr.

ILLUSTRATIONS

By Tasha Tudor

ARIEL BOOKS · NEW YORK

to HAL VURSELL,
*an editor who lives in the city
but whose mind often strays to the country*

© 1958 by Thomas L. McCready and Tasha Tudor.
Library of Congress catalog card no. 57-9634
*Published simultaneously in Canada
by Ambassador Books, Ltd.*
MANUFACTURED IN THE U. S. A.

INCREASE was the name of an enormous rabbit belonging to the four Warner children, of Webster, New Hampshire.

Bill, Emily, Ralph and Helen had so many pets they hardly needed more, but Mrs. Warner loved rabbits, and so she thought of course her children would enjoy owning a nice pair. And, to be sure, the children would take complete care of them, she said to herself, while she, Mrs. Warner, could love them all she pleased. This was a fine scheme, and it worked not only very well but a bit too well. It came about in this way:

A woman in the nearby town of Concord advertised Belgian hares for sale. Mrs. Warner went to see her.

"Please don't give me a male and a female," she said to the woman who was selling the

rabbits, "for I've heard how fast rabbits multiply. You may pick out either two males or two females, as you please, thank you."

The woman agreed to do as she was asked, and Mrs. Warner brought home two very fine males.

The rabbits were a soft, beautiful brown color, friendly and not at all afraid of people. The whole Warner family was delighted with the new pets. Their mother, the children said, certainly had a gift for buying just the right things!

They put the rabbits in a small, unused
chicken house, and each child agreed to feed
and care for their new pets in turn. And they
would have to find names for the rabbits, too.
The children discussed it for a few days and
finally decided on George and Albert as being nice names and easy to remember.

After the arrival of the rabbits, things settled down for a few weeks on the Warner farm. There was no particular excitement other than an occasional terrible cat fight between Mr. Stubbs, the Warners' tomcat with no tail, and a foolish neighboring cat or two who needed some first-rate cat discipline. Stubbs allowed no strange tomcats on Warner Farm. But this is a story about rabbits, not tomcats.

It must have been at least six weeks after the rabbits arrived when, one morning, it was Bill's turn to feed them. Hardly had he left with food and water than he was back at the house, and burst into the kitchen, breathless with excitement.

"Mother, the funniest thing is in the rabbit house! I've never seen anything like it. There's a pile of rabbit fur in one corner, and it moves.

I know George and Albert haven't been fighting. They aren't scratched up or chewed in any way and—well, come with me!"

Mr. and Mrs. Warner looked quickly at each other, but they said nothing. They ran after Bill as he flew back to the rabbits. Surely enough, there was a pile of rabbit fur.

"Pull away the top of that pile, Bill," ordered Mr. Warner. "I think there's something inside the fur."

"No! there may be a rat in there," said Bill. "You do it yourself, Pa!"

"All right," said Mr. Warner. "I'm not afraid of it, whatever it is!" And as he pulled away some of the fur, there lay in plain sight a cluster of seven fuzzy squirming creatures.

"Mice!" shouted Bill.

"No, you silly, those are baby rabbits," said
Mr. Warner. "That woman who sold your
mother two male rabbits was slightly mis-
taken. Albert and George are a father and a
mother and they have presented us with a
nice batch of babies. Isn't that exciting!"

"Oh my!" sighed Mrs. Warner in distress, "what are we to do now? Rabbits grow up in no time, and then the young ones will have babies just like these. I've forgotten my arithmetic but I do know rabbits multiply terribly fast."

"Well," said Mr. Warner, "it looks as if we will have to rename the rabbits. At least, one of them, for we can't go on calling Mrs. Rabbit George."

"I don't know," murmured Mrs. Warner in a worried tone. "Dear me, how they do *increase . . .*"

"Increase!" Bill exclaimed.

"Yes," said Emily with pleasure, "that is a pretty name!"

"I like it, too," said Ralph, and Helen, the youngest Warner child, said very slowly, "In—crease. Yes, that is a *very* nice name."

It mattered nothing to anyone that Increase was an old-fashioned name for a man, not meant for a woman or a mother rabbit. It fitted Mrs. Rabbit, and so the name stuck right to her, Increase Rabbit, wife of Albert.

The babies grew so fast it was almost possible to stand and watch them grow. Just as it is with kittens, it was not many days before they opened their eyes, and of course Increase was very busy nursing seven hungry little ones.

Albert didn't like his young ones at all.
Maybe it was because they took up so much
of his wife's time and attention; at any rate,
he was so very savage he was moved to tem-
porary quarters in the old milk-cooler room,
inside the barn. As for the tiny rabbits, they

refused to stay tiny or even babies very long. It was hard to keep up with each stage, so quickly did they develop. Eyes open one day, first shaky steps beyond the nest soon after, until soon they were weaned. Mr. Warner began to think it would soon be time to find a new home for all seven young rabbits. He meant to give them away rather than to try to sell them, but they were so sweet he kept putting off the day when he would take them away somewhere.

The Warner children all took regular turns
at farm chores, feeding livestock and pets, and
helping around the house. When it came time
for Helen to feed the rabbits, she was over-
joyed, for she adored them and had every in-
tention of taking wonderful care of them. But,
of all the children, she was the youngest and
most forgetful. Not being in the habit of clos-

ing doors around the house, she promptly for-
got to shut up the rabbit house the first morning she fed Increase and the seven small ones.

Mr. Warner came past an hour later and
found the door wide open. All the young rabbits were happily clustered about their feed
dish, but Increase was not in the rabbit pen.
"What now!" thought Mr. Warner, who
would have been almost glad to see the last
of such a problem. But he had what is called

a conscience, and so he began a thorough search for Increase. He dutifully shut the door on the little ones, but the thought did cross his mind that if they had escaped and disappeared for good and all, he wouldn't have the bother of giving them away. But, instead, it was Increase who was out, and she had to be found.

He looked all through the barn as well as beneath the hen house and out in the orchard, even as far as the vegetable garden where he imagined she might be found devouring some new lettuce plants. But no! There was not a trace of Increase anywhere. Mr. Warner began to get cross at his failure. He felt badly, too, at having to bring sad news to his family.

But, just as he came to the kitchen door, he was stopped by his wife who whispered to him to come quietly into the room. He tip-toed in through the door and was struck nearly dumb with amazement. There in the middle of the floor was none other than Increase Rabbit.

"Tell me please, dear, how you managed to catch this rabbit?"

"Catch it!" replied Mrs. Warner, "Increase came here and almost asked to come in. She was outside when I looked a while ago to see

what was keeping you so long, and she hopped in as though she belonged here. But I won't have her in my kitchen! Cats, dogs and children are enough! You might as well put her back with her little ones, if they haven't all escaped too. Have you seen them?"

Mr. Warner explained that the seven young ones were safe and sound, and he added he really must find them a new home as soon as possible.

Just then the children came in from their chores. They were thrilled to see Increase sitting comfortably in the kitchen and would not agree to let their father return her to her pen. They decided at once to train Increase to become a house pet.

"Four against two," they said to Mr. and
Mrs. Warner. "You'll have to let us train the
rabbit!"

"Five to one," said Mrs. Warner, voting
with the children. "On second thought it
would be a wonderful idea. What do you
think, Papa?"

"It will be all right with me," replied Mr.
Warner, "if you children wish to pay for whatever damage the so-called house rabbit may
do around this house. Just you wait and see!
I would advise against it, but go ahead and
have your own way."

The first thing of course was to housebreak Increase, that is to train her to use a sandbox just as the Warner tomcat, Mr. Stubbs, had been taught to do as a young kitten. She was by no means a tender young rabbit, but even so, she was quick enough to learn this necessary habit. And, once that was mastered, she made herself completely at home.

Indeed, Increase had ideas very much the same as those of her new friend Mr. Stubbs. They both had heavy fur coats and both were nocturnal animals, given to being more wide‑awake at night than in the daytime. Each of them loved to take long naps beneath the hot kitchen stove or, better still, to lie rabbit fashion before the open parlor fire so as to toast their whiskers. And they would lie this way side by side for hours at a time.

At night they would be wide awake. Mr. Stubbs would leave the house in search of tom‑cat pursuits around the buildings or in the fields and woods, but Increase was more than content to stay in the house. There, as a rule, she was quiet enough—and wise enough, too —not to disturb the sleeping Warner family.

But on occasion there were strange noises in the house during the night. They sounded very much like mice or rats at work. To be sure, Increase was a rodent, too, a very big one, and she did like to investigate and to chew on things. Along toward dawn one morning she got inside the kitchen scrap basket, and the commotion was enough to awaken Bill, the older Warner boy, a bit early that day. He came down from his room at the head of the back stairs expecting to find a large rat which Stubbs must have neglected to kill. Instead, he found Increase in the last stages of emptying the overturned basket. He was

careful to clean up the mess and not tell his father, who might chalk the incident up against Increase. This was not a serious offense but, to prevent its happening in the parlor or somewhere near enough to awaken Mr. Warner at night, Bill took to making sure the baskets in every room were emptied often, practically every day.

Increase's favorite sport, if any sport could be said to be preferred above all others, took place beneath the parlor sofa. Here she could hide without being seen, and from this wonderful observation post she could keep track of all cake and toast crumbs spilled by awkward children during the daily tea hour. So

thoroughly did she clean up all such crumbs
after teatime, she became invaluable to Mrs.
Warner who called her the best four-footed
vacuum cleaner in existence.

The Warners were modern farmers and their house had central heating and a large furnace in the cellar. In this cellar was the coal bin. Now Mrs. Warner hated this coal bin because so much soot and dirt was tracked up from it into her kitchen. But to Increase Rabbit the bin was irresistible. If ever anyone left open the door to the cellar, she was sure to know and to seize upon the chance to sneak down to a bit of real pleasure. There was simply no fun equal to trying to hop up a pile of loose coal, only to have it crumble and fall away in all directions, making lovely rattling sounds so pleasant to her ears. Not even the certain prospect of a bath given her by an irate Mrs. Warner was sufficient to stop Increase from enjoying the coal bin at any opportunity.

And if cats dislike a bath in a tub of soapy water, it is certain rabbits don't enjoy it a bit more. Poor Increase! It was pitiful to see her all bedraggled and wet, but she felt it was worth even such torture as the bath afterwards. Doubtlessly it was, or she'd have stayed out of the coal bin.

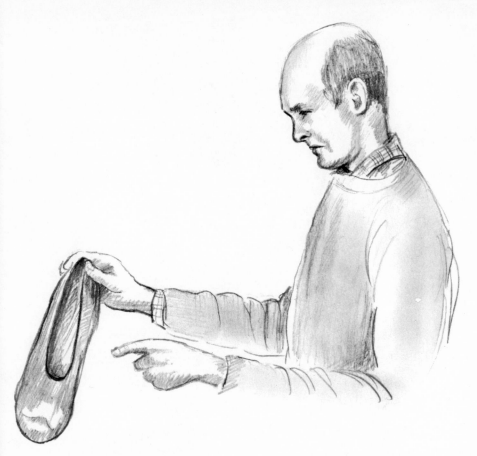

In general Increase was a very good rabbit. It is true that during the early stages of being housebroken, she seemed to prefer Mr. Warner's rubbers to using the sand in the rabbit box. This did not please Mr. Warner.

Nor was he pleased one stormy night when the wind howled so loudly no one could hear Increase tearing to shreds the seat of a fine rush-bottomed parlor chair. She was naughty, yes, but she was punished and never repeated that offense.

That does not mean Mrs. Warner's best straw bonnet did not tempt Increase two days before Easter Sunday. Nor did punishment for destroying the hat and chair seat teach her not to touch the wicker clothesbasket in the bathroom. But it is the nature of rabbits to

gnaw on things, and Increase was so charm-
ing it was hard to stay angry with her for long.

The boys taught Increase to tour the lawn
and gardens on a leash like a dog. She seemed
not to mind the leash and not even to suspect
that it was used because they didn't trust her
loose near the flower beds or the vegetable
garden. But she was always glad to get back
to the house, where she felt entirely at ease.
There were too many things outdoors which
might happen, at least that is what her rabbit instinct seemed to tell her. Things like
strange dogs suddenly appearing, or maybe
the cry of a distant hawk, would upset her. So
she never stayed out very long at a time.

Sometimes, before she came back to the house, Increase would be taken to visit Albert, who now lived again in the little red chicken house where his first family had been born. He seemed to find the house very much to his liking, especially after the bothersome young rabbits were finally given away. He spent absolutely his whole time in the little poultry house, usually with his paws crossed in front of him over the wooden roost. He did little else than sit in a half sitting, half standing position behind this roost where he could look through the wire door in front of

him. It was quite comical to watch him re-
move himself from this queer position at feeding time, or whenever something going on
around the yard made him curious enough
to want a better view from close to the door.
Certainly he wasn't much like his wife In-

crease, who was always active, doing something she considered good fun. To tell the
truth, Albert was a bit dull.

The Warner girls, Emily and Helen, enjoyed Increase in their own way just as much as the boys did in theirs. They spent hours trying baby clothes on the fat rabbit, who managed to wear them with considerable feminine stylishness. She would even wear a hat and ride in a doll carriage.

The Warners became so fond of Increase and told so many friends and neighbors of the wonders of a house rabbit, that the children soon had requests in the form of cash orders from small boys and girls who also wanted to own a superior rabbit.

Dear Emily and Helen please save me a baby rabbit from Increases next family. Here is my dollar. Love from Lucy

This resulted in a really wonderful decision. It was decided to allow Increase and Albert to have a family of babies every year. Nothing could have been more perfect. It was fair to the rabbits, who wanted children of their own. At least, Increase did, and in time even Albert seemed less bad-tempered when there were baby rabbits about.

It was profitable to the Warner boys and girls, who sold them and thus had money of their own, and it brought happiness to the children who bought the young rabbits.

And if anything were to happen either to Increase or Albert, it was always possible to

name a baby rabbit after its father or mother. And so the Warners were positively sure always to have either a new or an old edition of Increase or Albert Rabbit.